God Is with Me through the Day

written by Julie Cantrell

ZONDERkidz

ZONDERVAN.com/
AUTHORTRACKER
follow your favorite authors

God Is with Me Through the Day
Copyright © 2009 by Julie Cantrell

Requests for information should be addressed to:
Zonderkidz, *Grand Rapids, Michigan 49530*

Library of Congress Cataloging-in-Publication Data

Cantrell, Julie, 1973-
    God is with me through the day / by Julie Cantrell.
        p. cm.
    Summary: A child is reminded that God loves him all the time, even when he
is alone.
    ISBN-13: 978-0-310-71562-7 (hardcover)
    ISBN-10: 0-310-71562-8 (hardcover)
    [1. Christian life--Fiction. 2. Fear--Fiction.] I. Title.
    PZ7.C173566Gl 2009
    [E]--dc22
    {B}   2007022904

Published in association with the literary agency of WordServe Literary Group, LTD.,
10152 S. Knoll Circle, Highlands Ranch, Colorado 80130

Zonderkidz is a trademark of Zondervan.

Design: Jody Langley

Photo Credits:
Page 20: Thorsten Milse/Robert Harding World Imagery/Getty Images
Page 24: ©John W. Herbst/Corbis
Page 25: Martin Harvey/Gallo Images/Getty Images
Page 28: Wayne R Bilenduke/Stone/Getty Images

Printed in China

09 10 11 12 13 • 5 4 3 2 1

to Emily and Adam

In the morning

I wake up and stretch.

I laugh.

I play.

I am **happy** with my family.

I am **safe**

in my **home.**

Then Mama kisses
my cheek.

And
I run
out
the
door.

I start to feel alone.

I try to be brave.

But
sometimes
I cry.

I feel very small in the great big world.

That's when I remember that
God is always with me.

Just like when he helped

David fight the lions

to save his sheep.

Just like when God kept Jonah
safe inside the whale.

When I'm afraid,
I say
out loud,

"God loves me."

I roar like a bear,
    " I am safe!"

My world doesn't seem so
scary anymore.

In God's
hands,
I am
strong.

I am loved!

And I am **never**

alone.

"When I am
afraid,
I will
trust
in you."

—Psalm 56:3